Arthur Evans Moule

Chinese Stories for Boys and Girls

And Chinese Wisdom for Old and Young

Arthur Evans Moule

Chinese Stories for Boys and Girls
And Chinese Wisdom for Old and Young

ISBN/EAN: 9783337168483

Printed in Europe, USA, Canada, Australia, Japan

Cover: Foto ©Andreas Hilbeck / pixelio.de

More available books at **www.hansebooks.com**

CHINESE STORIES

FOR BOYS AND GIRLS

AND

CHINESE WISDOM FOR OLD AND YOUNG

EDITED AND TRANSLATED BY
ARTHUR E. MOULE, B.D.
C.M.S. MISSIONARY TO NINGPO AND HANGCHOW, CHINA

WITH TEN ENGRAVINGS

SEELEY, JACKSON, & HALLIDAY, FLEET STREET
LONDON. MDCCCLXXXI

PREFACE.

A CHINESE story-book lies before me. It is in two volumes, containing in all one hundred and two stories, with a picture to illustrate each tale. This is a very popular work in China, and many editions are published by rich people for free distribution. I am acquainted with the gentleman in Hangchow who superintended the cutting of the blocks for this edition. Anyone who can make the journey to Hangchow and will apply at the publishing office, can have a copy gratis, or at mere cost price, if he prefers to pay.

I give to my readers a few specimens of these stories. They all have one object, namely, the illustration of filial and fraternal duties.

The plates in this little book are fac-simile copies of the outline illustrations in the Chinese original.

CONTENTS.

CHINESE STORIES.

CHAPTER I.

ALLOW me to introduce to you two hundred millions and more of Chinese boys and girls.

I must not attempt to give you all their names. That would take too long altogether. I can only mention one or two, and my readers must imagine the rest.

Here comes Master " Long-lived King," and Master " Glorious Light Summer." Here is Miss " Beautiful Gem Place," and Miss " Beautiful Phœnix Bell." Then there are nicknames, and pet names, and the babies have what the Chinese call " milk-names,"

like our "Tiny," "Dot," and so on. But
the superstitious Chinese, being afraid of the
evil eye, and of calamity following if they
choose too high-sounding names, often call
their children by some mean title, in order
to avoid the envy of evil spirits. So one is
called "Little Dog," and another "Hill Dog,"
"Old Cow," and so on. These milk-names
and nicknames sometimes cling to them
through life. A tailor whom we employed
in Ningpo was called "Dog the Tailor."

But a mother's love and pride often over-
come these foolish fears, and "The Precious
One" is a common name for a little girl or
boy; or "Threefold Happiness," meaning
"much joy, many sons, much money"—the
Chinese ideal of threefold or perfect bliss.
Sometimes convenience guides the selection
of names, and the child is called simply
"Number One," "Number Five," and so
on. Then, when the boys go to school (there
are no schools for girls except mission
schools in China), they have a *book-name*
selected by the master, and written on the

class books and copy slips : such as, " Perfect Talent," " Pervading Excellence," etc.

I fancy that English children suppose all Chinese children to be very odd and strange beings. And I am sorry to say that Chinese children are taught to speak of English children as being very curious beings indeed. But as we go to China to try and teach the Chinese children better, so should I be glad if I can give to English children truer ideas about the Chinese.

What do these children, with their little pigtails, eat ? you will ask me. Is not cat or dog their usual dish ? It may be so sometimes. You may have heard the old story of an English gentleman who was invited to a dinner-party in a Chinese gentleman's house. He could not speak Chinese well ; so being doubtful as to a dish which was set before him, he pointed to the dish, and then turned to his host, and asked, " Quack, quack ?" which plainly meant, " Is this duck ?" The host shook his head, and, using the same language, replied, " Bow-

wow !"—plainly meaning, " No, it is dog."
The notice " Black cat always ready," may be
seen, I believe, in a butcher's shop at Canton.

Another curious dish which is sometimes
prepared for honoured guests is " ducks'
tongues."

But we must remember that very curious
things are eaten in England sometimes.
Many a rabbit-pie is suspected of having
mewed when alive.

Except in times of famine, such as have
lately devastated five of the provinces,
causing the death of about seven millions of
people, the Chinese have very good food.
Indeed a Chinese nurse who has come with
us to England recommends English servants
to emigrate to China, because she thinks
Chinese vegetables and fruits so much better
than those in England. I don't agree with
her there ; but really some of the vegetables
in China are very good ; and I will describe
one of these, because it will be mentioned
more than once in the stories which I have
translated for your amusement. This vege-

table is the young shoots of the *bamboo*. The
bamboo is one of the most beautiful and
valuable of trees. It grows very rapidly.
Shoots come up from the roots of the old
bamboos early in April; and pushing
through the soft earth like great asparagus
(only much thicker, and hard and firm instead of soft), they reach their full height—
that is to say, from twenty to thirty feet—by
July; and year after year they grow no
taller, but the hollow stem hardens its rind.
This hard stem is turned to every imaginable
use. The masts, and sails, and ropes, and
poles, and tilts of ships and boats are made
of bamboo. Rain-shoots, and chairs, and
tables, and chop-sticks (the Chinaman's
knife and fork), and cups and bowls, all come
from this wonderful tree; and you often see
a Chinaman at his dinner eating boiled
bamboo-shoots, with bamboo chop-sticks in
his hand, and a bamboo vessel or basket of
boiled rice supplying his chief dish.*

* The following clever piece of verse was written by
Major Arthur T. Bingham Wright, and answers admirably

You will meet with men and women, as
well as with boys and girls, in the stories

the double purpose of describing the uses of the bamboo-
tree, and also of illustrating the peculiarities of the
strange jargon called Pidgin-English—a language in-
vented in China as a means of communication between
English or Americans and the natives. "*Pidgin*" seems
to be a Chinese attempt at pronouncing the word "business;" and it certainly is used now for "business."
Pidgin-English is, in fact, distorted English words
arranged according to Chinese order and idiom :

John Chinaman's Lignum Vitæ.

1.

One piecee thing that my have got,
Maskee that thing my no can do,
You talkey you no sabey what ?
     Bamboo.

2.

That chow chow all too muchee sweet
My likee ; what no likee you ?
You makee try, you makee eat
     Bamboo.

3.

That olo house too muchee small,
My have got chilo, wanchee new ;
My makee one big piecee, all
     Bamboo.

4.

Top-side that house my wanchee thatch,
And bottom-side that matting too ;
My makee both if my can catch
     Bamboo.

which follow. Some of their customs are much more curious than their eating and drinking. They are very careful about the

---

5.

That sun he makee too much hot,
My makee hat (my talkee true)
And coat for rain ; if my have got
    Bamboo.

6.

That Pilong too much robbery
He makee ; on his back one, two,
He catchee for his bobbery
    Bamboo.

7.

No wanchee walk that China pig,
You foreigner no walkee you,
My carry both upon a big
    Bamboo.

8.

What makee Sampan go so fast ?
That time the wind so strong he blew,
What makee sail and rope and mast ?
    Bamboo.

9.

My catchee every thing in life
From number one of trees that grew,
So muchee good I give my wife
    Bamboo.

10.

And now Man-man, my talkee done,
And so my say chin-chin to you ;
My hope you think this number one
    Bamboo.

burial of the dead ; and they think, as the Greeks and Romans thought of old, that if a person is not properly buried, his soul will be very uncomfortable, and perhaps try to take revenge on those who have neglected the funeral rites. The Chinese buy very large and thick coffins when they can afford it, the planks being six inches thick sometimes. They seal and plaster down the lid, and often keep the dear departed in the house or in a temple for days and months, or even years, till a lucky day has come for the funeral.

Those who have money buy their coffins when they are quite well and strong, and keep them in the house. You will remember that Nelson had a coffin given him by one of his captains, made out of the mainmast of the French ship *L'Orient* (Casabianca's ship), and he kept this in his state-room on board the *Victory*.

Twenty years ago, during the war and confusion in China, caused by the rising of the " Long-haired " Rebels, our washerman came one day to ask if he might deposit at our house his most valuable property. We

consented; and the next day he brought a
number of thick, well-seasoned planks.
They were to make his mother's coffin;
though the old lady was alive and well, and
lived for some years afterwards.

An old beggar woman, who had scraped
together a good deal of money, was afraid
that the rebel soldiers would steal her little
store; so she hid the dollars for safety in her
coffin, which she had bought and kept in her
hovel. Then she sat down by its side, pre-
tending to be in abject poverty and misery.
Unhappily for the old woman a neighbour
had seen this through a chink in the wall, and
led the soldiers in and shared in the spoils.
Then the poor old woman in despair left
the city, and soon afterwards died. "Where
her treasure was, there was her heart;" and
those who set their affections on things below
do but place their treasures in the grave.

The Chinese think that at death our souls
break up into three; and that one soul goes
into the unseen world for judgment, one
goes to live in the tablet—a piece of wood
called "the throne of the soul" which is

worshipped by the children of the dead—and one goes to stay with the corpse in the coffin.

But strange as Chinese customs are, I think you will agree with me when you have read the stories in this book, that those who are taught to love their parents, and to reverence and respect their elders, are not people to be laughed at or despised; but that English boys and girls may learn a good many lessons from them.

Well, you will ask me, if this is so, why do you go out to preach to them? For this reason—a reason which you will gather also from the stories which follow. In the first place, the Chinese do not act up even to their dim light, nor practise what they preach so well. Then again, the Chinese commit two great sins. They forget God, and they remember man instead of God. They have gods many, and lords many, it is true; like a family with many heads, or a kingdom with many kings (a shame and a crime in Chinese eyes). But "the God in Whose hand their breath is" they forget, and daily sin against. Then, besides their many idols, they turn dead men and women into deities. One of the sayings of Confucius, their great teacher, who lived between B.C. 551 and 478, was " He who places his forefathers on an equality with heaven, and sacrifices to his father as he sacrifices to God, performs the greatest of all moral duties."

Thus they "leave the fountain of living waters, and hew out to themselves cisterns, broken cisterns, that can hold no water."— Jer. ii. 13.

The Chinese speak of the five great relations.

(1) The duty of ministers and their prince.

(2) The duty of children and their father.

(3) The duties of husband and wife.

(4) The duty of brother to brother.

(5) The duty of friend to friend.

Now, as you will find in the stories which follow, the Chinese would think very little of the man who was kind to his friend and was unkind to his brother ; or of the woman who loved her brother and deserted her husband ; or of the husband who loved his wife and neglected his parents; or of the man who was dutiful to his parents and rebelled against his emperor.

And so, out of their own mouths, they are judged. They neglect or forget their duty towards God; and no other virtue or excellence can make up for this. They need therefore the knowledge of the only True God, and of Jesus Christ whom He has sent; the blessed doctrine of a Father, Redeemer, and Sanctifier. And this salvation we preach to them at the commandment of the Lord Jesus Christ.

Yet, notwithstanding their sins and strange customs and follies, there is much, as I said before, to admire in the Chinese; and I hope that these stories will interest my readers as showing how the Chinese *think*, and how *human* they are; and therefore how well worth the while it is for English Christians to spend their money and their lives in doing good to this great people. " Within the four seas "—that is, everywhere, said Confucius, "all men are brethren."

CHAPTER II.

BEFORE opening the door, and asking you in to listen to the stories which the Chinese love to hear, I must tell you a little more about the customs and habits of Chinese children.

In China boys are considered much more valuable than girls. This arises partly from the fact that girls are betrothed very early, and sometimes go to live in their future mother-in-law's house long before they are married, being lost thus to their own parents. Then again sons will, it is hoped, continue the family name, and perform the sacrifices and worship at the graves of their dead parents and ancestors. A Chinese proverb calls good girls " Fine bamboo-shoots springing up *outside* the fence," bringing happiness and good ; that is, outside the old home and to another family. So, when a son is born, there are very loud and joyful congratulations. When a girl comes, the best thing that friends can say is, " Well ! girls also are of some use!"

In certain districts of China, and especially when famine or war prevails, the poor people destroy their little girls as soon as they are born. But this is not so common a crime as is often supposed. In Ningpo there is a society formed by the heathen gentry to suppress this crime. They have agents in different parts of the country who give help in money to poor parents when a girl is born, and punish those who allow their infants to be destroyed. I heard once of a poor man who had *eleven* daughters born one after another; and when the eleventh little thing came, he was in despair, and allowed the poor baby to be drowned. Upon which the agent of this society pounced down upon him, and he was punished severely for his crime.

In the north of China, where I have lived for many years, the summers are very hot, and the winters are very cold. The little children are scarcely clothed at all in July and August, but are nearly smothered with clothes in the winter. Little cotton trousers and jackets, or sometimes gauze tunics, are all that they can bear for *full* dress in the great heat; and they would never sleep at all in their low close houses during the sultry summer nights, with myriads of mosquitoes buzzing round, but for the kind care of their mothers fanning them to sleep.

The Chinese in the Chehkiang Province have no fire-places or stoves for *warmth* in the winter; and they light fires merely for cooking; so that the only way to keep the children warm is to put on more and more clothes as the weather grows colder and colder. The poor people use cotton clothes wadded with cotton wool; and the richer people wear fur-lined garments. The little children in mid-winter, with their thick wadded jackets on, look like bolsters ; or when *very* small, like balls.

Almost every village has its school, and rich and poor children go to the same school. Rich people, however, have private tutors for their elder boys ; and sometimes, though very rarely, the girls are taught to read and write as well as the boys, though they never go to a school. In many places there are charity schools endowed by some rich man. The fees in boys' schools vary in different places; but the average is much the same as in England—that is to say, from three half-pence a week for young children, up to five-pence for elder pupils ; and the parents of the children have to provide their school-books, and sometimes to supply their stools and tables as well. What is generally called the three R's in England, is reduced to two in Chinese schools—namely, reading and writing alone ; and they learn everything by heart, getting accustomed to the shape and sound of their strange written and printed words, and not

learning the *meaning* of what they are taught till they are thirteen or fourteen years old. There is no *alphabet* in Chinese, but every word has a sign or picture to itself; and the right spelling of the word is the right number and position of the strokes and dots which compose it. So that school life is rather dull for the little boys when they begin. They do not learn arithmetic at school, or geography, or the history of any other country except China, and not much about China even; neither do they learn botany, or astronomy, or geology. They are quick enough in money matters, indeed, and can add up sums very fast; but they do this with the *abacus* or counting-board. The girls are taught at home to cook and to sew, and to embroider, and in rich houses to play the guitar. They are employed, when very young, in weaving silk, and especially, alas! in making gold and silver tinsel paper, which is used in the worship of the idols or of ancestors. The schoolmasters sometimes punish naughty boys with a flat ruler; but the most usual punishment is to make the culprit kneel down in disgrace, or kneel up on a stool for a long time.

English boys and girls, with their play-grounds and indoor and outdoor games, would wonder how Chinese children can ever be happy with their very few and poor amusements. No cricket; no football; no hockey; no boating or yachting; no hunt-the-slipper or blind-man's-buff (though the Chinese have some idea of this last game). The children, however, do not look sad at all. They laugh and shout, and they enjoy their Punch-and-Judy shows (which some people suppose to have been introduced into England from China), and their fireworks at the new year, and their paper and clay toys, and the rattles for the baby, and their shuttle-cocks knocked about with the heels and soles of their shoes, instead of a battle-dore; and their toy lanterns (paper figures of horses, some of them on wheels, with a red candle lit inside), and above all, their kite-flying in the spring-time. It is an odd sight, however, to see old grey-headed men enjoying this amusement as much as the children. On a mild, breezy day in February or March, the old gentlemen will come out, and, when the kite has been sent up by the boys, they will sit down on a bamboo chair by the hour holding the string and guiding the kite. These kites are of all shapes— some like butterflies or beetles ; some like a dragon, or a centipede ; some like an eagle. Some are in the form of the sign for a word,

as, for instance 日 *sun;* or 春 *spring.* They have kites also with lanterns fastened to their tails, which burn for a long time, and look very pretty, like steady meteors in the dark night sky.

Chinese children are as fond of sweets as English children ; and sugar-candy is to be bought in their shops, with red and yellow sweets of different kinds. They are very fond also of sucking sugar-cane.

The women and girls wear fragrant flowers in their hair, and the men and boys also will sometimes stick sprigs of sweet flowers into the upper plaits of their queues, or *pig-tails*, as we foreigners mischievously call them.

In the early spring, when a sweet-smelling orchid called *lan-hwa* comes out, almost every house has a pot of this flower in the window. And in the early autumn, when the delicious *olea fragrans* blooms, sprigs are sold in the streets, and everyone wears it.

But the Chinese have nothing to be compared with our flower-gardens; no broad lawns, or deep rich flower-beds, or screens of laurel and laurestinus. Chinese gardens are very small, and consist chiefly of artificial rock work and trees, cut and bent into fantastic shapes. It is a pleasant sight, therefore, once or twice a year, to see the poor women and children going off into the country to breathe the fresh air, and to mount the hills. They come back in the evening with bright red azalea blossoms in their hair, and branches of it (gathered wild on the hills) in the boat's head. But it is sad to think that this their one "day in the country " is spared and planned with the sole object of visiting the tombs of their dead friends and worshipping their spirits. The Chinese care much less than we do for *wild* flowers; and the banks of their rivers and canals, which are covered with a carpet of clover and small buttercups in the spring time, never seem to please the children as they would in England.

I spoke of boats just now. This is the usual way of travelling in a great part of China, because the country is cut up and crossed by rivers and canals in all directions. These boats are not rowed with two or four oars or more at the side, as with us, but are sculled by one long oar (or sometimes with as many as four) at the stern.

There are also small fast boats, sometimes called by foreigners snake-boats, I suppose from their wriggling motion. The Chinese call them " foot-rowed boats," from the fact that they are rowed by one long oar grasped and pulled, and *feathered* too, by the boatman's feet, as he sits leaning against an upright board at the stern, whilst he steers and steadies the boat with a short paddle under his arm. These boats are very narrow and cranky, and the passenger has to lie down during his journey, or at most sit upon his bedding, spread on the bottom of the boat. In the larger passenger-boats (some of which will carry as many as thirty or forty people), mattresses and coverlets are spread on movable boards fitted across the hinder part of the boat like an upper deck, whilst tables and chairs are arranged on the boards of the lower deck. Most of these boats are fitted with tilts made of split bamboo plaited together. Cooking goes on in the boatmen's quarters in the stern. In the hill country and in the cities, those who can afford it travel about in sedan-chairs.

Many of the Chinese are *very* poor, especially perhaps those who live in boats all the year round, and earn their livelihood by fishing in the canals. I have often seen a family of seven or eight at home in a boat not more than ten feet long and four feet six

inches wide.   In fine weather, when the little
ones can bask in the sun or run on the banks,
it is all very well; but in winter time, with
snow and rain, it must be a miserable life
indeed, cooped up in this wet and filthy
dwelling.

The poor, however, seldom take to *begging*.
Beggars, indeed, swarm in China, and are
governed by a kind of gipsy king; but they
are professional beggars, and follow their
calling from choice.   Some rich people found
charities in China.   Soup kitchens are opened,
and rice is distributed to poor widows; and
there are almshouses and foundling hospitals,
not well managed, it is true, but set on foot,
I dare say, with a kind intention.

Children get ill in China as well as in England; but they have not such tender nurses
and skilful doctors as we have.   Measles, and
chicken-pox, and small-pox, and fevers, and a
kind of whooping cough, and cholera, and
dysentery—these are common diseases in
China; but there is very little scarlet-fever,
which is so much dreaded in England, or

yellow-fever, which is so bad in the West Indies and in the southern states of America.

Alas! that neither Chinese men and women, nor boys and girls, know anything of that better land, of which the Bible tells us :

"Sorrow and death may not enter there."

" From a child " they know only how to worship idols and ancestors. Family parties may often be seen in the temples ; grand-mothers and mothers teaching the little ones to bow down to idols. Here is a description given by an eye-witness, Dr. Yates of Shanghai in China.

He used to wonder why almost everyone in China is an idolater, and he found that the Chinese wondered themselves, because they could not remember the time when they did *not* worship idols.

One day Dr. Yates discovered the reason. He was introduced into an idol-temple, and stood in the back part of the great hall, where the chief idols are placed for worship ; and from thence he could watch what went forward.

Soon a well-dressed lady came in with her three children, of about seven, five, and three years of age. The two elder boys ran forward and bowed down before the idol in the usual way, and then called their little brother to come forward also and do as they had done. But this was evidently his first visit to the temple, for the little fellow was very much frightened at the sight of the idol. The mother then dragged her child into position, and standing behind him and holding him fast by both arms, forced him to bow slightly three times; and then adroitly slipped out of her sleeve some toys and sweets, which she gave the child, saying that the god had given him these nice things because he was a good boy; and she told him to thank the idol, which he did.

A fortnight later Dr. Yates was in his place again. (The first and fifteenth of each month are the great days for worship.) Soon the mother with her three children appeared. The little boy was not so frightened as on the former occasion. He went up in front of the idol by himself, and said to his mother, "I don't know how to do it." He was assisted and rewarded as before; and from that day that child was an *idolater.* "The fright and the presents," as Dr. Yates says, "had welded the chain."

Now it is to break this chain that our Mission schools and other Mission agencies are set on foot; and I have selected and translated the following stories in order to increase the interest of my readers in the Chinese, who are bound thus hand and foot by superstition and idolatry, though free and eager in their fancies and aspirations.

CHAPTER III.

I.

THE parents of Tsze-loo, the favourite disciple of Confucius, were poor ; and he himself was in the habit of eating nothing but herbs and pulse, while he carried rice for his parents on his back thirty miles and more.

When the old people died, Tsze-loo travelled southwards to the country of Ts'oo, a hundred carts following him loaded with ten thousand measures of grain. When he arrived at the grave, he spread his mat, and sat down upon it, and then set up his three-legged kettle, and ate his meal ; and, sighing, said :

"Though I am willing to eat herbs and

3—2

pulse, and to carry grain for my parents to eat, alas, they are not!"

If then a son thus longs to support and help his parents when they are gone, is it not strange that sons living by their parents' side, with the joy and blessing of their presence, will not seize this opportunity for dutiful service?

II.

In the Chow Dynasty (about three thousand years ago) there was a man named Laou Lai-tsze. When he was seventy years of age he used to put on bright and many-coloured clothes; and then he would play about like a child. Sometimes he would carry water into the hall, and pretend to stumble, and fall flat on the ground; and then he would cry, and run up to his parents' side to please the old people, and all to make them forget, for a time at least, their own great age.

III.

There was once a man named Han. When he was a boy he misbehaved him-

self very often, and his mother used to
beat him with a bamboo-rod. One day he
cried after the beating, and his mother was
greatly surprised, and said :

" I have beaten you many a time, and
you have never cried before ; why do you
cry to-day ?"

" Oh, mother !" he replied, " you used to
hurt me when you flogged me ; but now I
weep because you are not strong enough to
hurt me."

" It makes one weep," says the Chinese
moralist, "even to read this story." Who
does not long to have the dear vanished
hand back again, and the still voice speaking
again, if even to punish and reprove ?

IV.

There was once a man named Yin-tsze,
who was very dutiful to his father and
mother.

When they were old they both became
stone blind. One day they took it into
their heads that they would like to taste
deer's milk. So Yin-tsze, wishing to gratify

them, put on a deer's-skin and horns and
crept in amongst a herd of deer, and managed
to secure some milk. Just then some hunts-
men came up, and were going to shoot
Yin-tsze; but he shouted out in time, and
told them who he was, and so escaped.

V.

About eighteen hundred years ago there
was a man named Ong, who, when a child, lost
his father, and lived alone with his mother.

Civil war broke out, and he carried his
mother off on his back to escape the confusion. Many a time, when he was out
searching for some food for his mother, he
met the banditti, who seized him and threatened to drag him off. But he wept, and
told them of his old mother at home depend-
ing on him; and even these rough robbers
had not the heart to kill him.

VI.

About eighteen hundred years ago there
was a man named Mao, who entertained a
friend, one Koh, and kept him to spend the
night. Early on the following morning Mao

killed a fowl for breakfast, and Mr. Koh
flattered himself that it was for *him*. But
no! it was for Mao's old mother; and Mao
and Koh sat down to nothing but greens
and rice. When Koh saw this he rose up
from the table, bowed low to Mao, and said:

"Well done, illustrious man!"

There is plenty of cordiality amongst
friends in the world, but too much neglect of
parents. This example of old Mao's teaches
us the right order of duties.

VII.

There was once a little boy named Loh
Tsih, or "Laudable Highland."

When he was six years old, in the city of
Kew-kiang he met a gentleman named Ze,
who gave him two oranges. Young "Laudable" popped them into his bosom, and then,
remembering himself, he turned round and
bowed his thanks. But as he bowed, the
oranges rolled out on to the ground. Ze
exclaimed:

"Here's a pretty young visitor, to hide
his oranges and carry them off without eating
them! What does this mean?"

" Laudable " knelt down before the great gentleman and said :

" My mother is particularly fond of oranges, and I wish to keep them for *her*."

Ze was greatly astonished, and let him go.

VIII.

A man named Lee was very dutiful to his mother. She was naturally a very nervous woman, and always dreadfully frightened in a thunderstorm.

When she died Lee buried his dear mother in a wood; and whenever the wind arose and a tempest threatened, he ran to the tomb, knelt down, and with tears cried out :

" Lee is near you—don't be afraid, mother!"

IX.

There was a boy once named Woo Mang, or " Brave and Talkative." When only eight years old he was very dutiful to his parents.

They were very poor, and could not afford even mosquito-curtains* for their bed in the summer. So their little boy used to get

---

* Mosquitoes are gnats which sting so badly, especially at night, that all but the very poor in China have gauze or net bed-curtains to keep them out.

into his parents' bed early in the evening, and let the mosquitoes do their worst at biting him for an hour or two ; and then, when they were surfeited with his blood, and fatigued with their venomous exertions, he got out and called to his parents to sleep in peace.

X.

About seven hundred years ago, a poor man went into the field with his little daughter " Fragrance " to cut maize.

Suddenly a tiger rushed out and dragged him off. " Fragrance " had no weapon of any kind in her hand. She knew only that she had a father ; and she forgot that she had a body. So she leapt forward, and seized the tiger by his throat, which gnashed its teeth and died, and the man escaped.

XI.

About sixteen hundred years ago, in time of confusion, a general named Woo collected an army and made head against the rebels. He had only just recovered from an abscess on his back, and in consequence of his energy and exertions he died. His two sons who accompanied him fell by the hand of the enemy.

" Home they brought her warriors dead ;" and the mother laid her hand gently on the corpses and wept, and said : " The father was a loyal officer, and the boys were dutiful sons. Come, come, no time for lamentation now !"

The death on one day of father and sons seems the greatest of sorrows ; but for faithful and dutiful conduct to spring up side by side like tufted grass, this is the greatest of joys.

XII.

A man named Chung lost his father in early childhood ; and his mother, when old, fell ill, and longed for some bamboo-shoots to eat. Chung could not find any, because the ground was dry and hard. He went to the wood, leant against the trees, and wept. His tears fell like rain, and moistened the ground, so that the shoots sprang up instantly, and with joy he took them to his mother.

XIII.

About thirteen hundred years ago an officer was unjustly accused of treason by a brother officer, and was condemned to death. His son, who was only fifteen years of age, went in boldly and beat the drum to claim an audience, entreating to be allowed to die for his father.

The emperor thereupon set the man free; and then expressed his intention of giving the boy the title " Perfectly Dutiful."

The boy exclaimed : " It is right and just for a son to die when his father is disgraced ; but what disgrace can be compared with the idea of gaining honour at a father's expense ? I respectfully decline your majesty's proposed distinction."

XIV.

A certain man had a mother who lost her sight, and he spent all his money on doctors, but in vain. For thirty long years he cared for his mother, and would scarcely take off his clothes; and in the pleasant spring weather he would lead his mother into the garden, and laugh and sing, so that his mother forgot her sadness.

When she died her son wasted away from grief; and when at last he somewhat recovered his health, he loved his brothers and sisters like his mother, and was as gentle to his nephews and nieces as if they had been his own children. As he said himself: "This is the only way in which I can get some comfort, namely, in letting my love go forth to those who are left."

XV.

A great officer named Yang served his mother most dutifully.

In the springtime he used to carry his mother up and down on his back amongst the wealth of flowers; and he would frisk and gambol about, while his mother enjoyed the fragrance and the shade.

The old lady died at the age of one hundred and four.

XVI.

The eldest son of an ancient emperor had a younger brother, whose name meant " Junior

Order," who again had a son named "Illustrious," a lad of remarkable ability. When the elder brother knew that his father's intention was to bequeath the throne to "Junior Order" and "Illustrious," he and the second son, "Harmony," sought a livelihood by collecting medicinal herbs, and went off to the barbarous tribes of China. Moreover, they shaved their heads and tatooed their skin, as much as to say, "We are no longer possible candidates for the throne."

By thus secretly ascertaining his father's wishes, and departing at once with his second brother, there was no trace left of the somewhat roundabout arrangement between father, sons, and brothers. In all these matters we should avoid the straight and stiff following of our own inclinations.

XVII.

A prince whose name meant "Solitary Bamboo" had three sons. He left directions in his will that the youngest son should succeed him. But the younger brother wished to make way for the elder. The elder re-

plied, " It is our father's order," and forthwith disappeared. The younger refused the
throne and left the country, like his elder
brother, and the people of the land elected
the second son as their prince. This mutual
yielding of Yee and Tsee, or " Even " and
" Equal," as they were called, was used by
Confucius as a theme for the exposition of
the word *benevolence*—for yielding springs
from benevolence, and benevolence is per-
fected by yielding. Yet people of this later
age seem to think yielding some great affair,
or a method for gaining a good reputation,
instead of letting it spring up as the outflow
of a wide and large heart.

Such things as "boiling the bean "* are
flatly contrary to benevolence.

* "Boiling the bean" refers to a celebrated poet
named Ts'ao Chih, who lived from A.D. 192—232. He
was the third son of the great Ts'ao Ts'ao, the most pro-
minent character in the great drama of Chinese history
forming the epoch known as that of the three kingdoms.
His elder brother, who succeeded to the throne on the
death of his father, Ts'ao Ts'ao, was jealous of his younger
brother's talent, and in order to bring him to confusion,
commanded him, under threat of punishment, to compose

XVIII.

There was once a man named Meaou Yung. He was left an orphan in early life. He was the eldest of four brothers, who lived together, holding their property in common, until each brother took to himself a wife, and then the women began to clamour for a division of the property, and there was constant bickering and contention.

Yung was deeply grieved; but instead of upbraiding his brothers and sisters-in-law, he went into his room, shut the door, and beat his breast, saying :

" Meaou Yung, Meaou Yung, you talk of regulating your person and acting with caution, and imitating the sages of old ; how comes it, then, that you cannot regulate your own household, I should like to know ?"

---

an ode while taking seven paces. Ts'ao Chih obeyed as follows :

" A kettle had beans inside,
    And stalks of the bean made the fire ;
  When the beans to their brother stalks cried,
    ' We spring from one root—why such ire ?' "
      See MAYER's *Chinese Reader's Manual*, p. 229.

His brothers and their wives heard what he was saying, and they at once confessed their faults, and were happier and more peaceable together than ever.

XIX.

There was once a mandarin named Soo. He had under his jurisdiction a person named Yih or " Bent."

This man quarrelled with his brothers about some land, and went to law. Year after year the case dragged on; each party brought forward fresh evidence, and a hundred persons were involved in the lawsuit. The prefect at last summoned " Bent " and his brothers before him and addressed them as follows :

" It is difficult to get a brother, it is easy enough to get land. Suppose you gain your fields and lose your brother, how will you feel then ?"

The prefect wept, and none of the bystanders could restrain their tears. The brothers then bowed low to the magistrate and asked his pardon, and reflecting on their sad ten years of quarrels and separation, at once resumed their common dwelling.

XX.

Kiang Ong's family was renowned for filial piety and brotherly love. When they were children, he and his two brothers slept under the same coverlet, with exceeding great love and harmony ; and when they were grown up, their love could not bear a moment's separation.

On one occasion they met with robbers, and the brothers strove for death, each one wishing to die first, with the hope of the others escaping. The robbers, seeing this, released them all three.

XXI.

There was once a man named Chen Kwan. His elder brother was a petty officer under the district magistrate, and secretly received bribes. Kwan, or " Just," as his name means, reproved his brother, but he paid no attention. " Just " thereupon went away and became a common labourer, and after a year, having saved a sum of money and bought some silk, he gave it to his brother, saying:

"When your goods are stolen or your money exhausted, they can be recovered again; but for an officer to take bribes is to ruin himself for life."

His brother, moved by "Just's" conduct, forthwith became virtuous and clean-handed.

XXII.

One Tien, or "Field," and his two brothers were discussing the division of their property. In front of the hall there was a Judas tree, and they consulted as to dividing the tree also into three parts. The tree forthwith withered away and died. "Field" said to his brothers:

"The tree with its one root withered away when it heard that it was to be divided.

"Surely men are not to be compared to wood!"

Upon this they became exceedingly sad, and they all resolved to live together again. And so they did, and were more friendly and loving than ever.

The Judas tree also flourished afresh.

XXIII.

There was a man named Sih Pao, both clever and good. His father, influenced by the stepmother, took a dislike to Pao, and turned him out of doors. Pao wept day and night, and could not bear to leave; but whenever he ventured in again his father beat him. Pao then made a shed outside the house, and came in early in the morning, and sprinkled the floor and swept it clean.

His father flew into a rage, and drove him out again. Then Pao put up his shed further off, just outside the court gate; and morning and evening never omitted his visits to inquire after his parents' welfare. After this had gone on for a year or more, his father and mother were ashamed of themselves, and restored him to his home.

Pao's nephew (some years after), being the only surviving member of the family, proposed to divide the property and live apart. Pao, much as he regretted this, could not prevent it; so he divided the goods into two shares and claimed the first choice. Of the

men servants and women servants he chose
the elderly ones, saying, " I can't send away
those who have long worked with me."
From the fields and farm-buildings he
selected the waste and crazy, saying, " These
are what I tended when a boy; I have a
fancy for them still." From the household
utensils and clothing he chose the rotten and
worn-out ones, remarking, " These are what
I used to eat from, these I used to wear;
they once pleased my mouth and my body :
they shall do so still."

His nephew was a spendthrift, and wasted
his patrimony ; but Pao made it up for him
again.

XXIV.

A man named Hien was renowned for his
filial and fraternal piety.

His brother was sick, fell into a trance, and
seemed to die.   He came to life again, however; but for some months after his recovery he
could not speak. Hien attended on his brother
himself, fed him, and nursed him, and did not
leave the house-door for thirteen years.

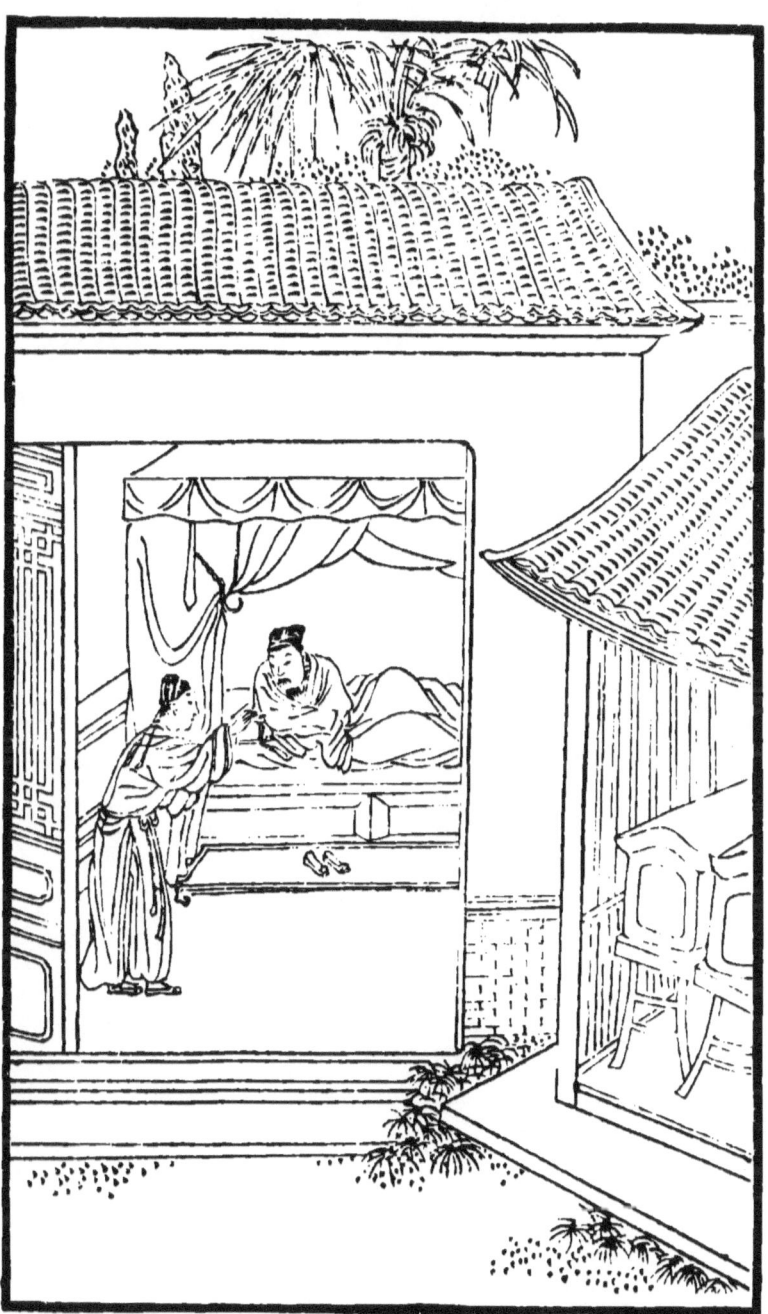

XXV.

During the Tsin dynasty (about fourteen hundred years ago) a great pestilence swept over the land. Two brothers of a certain family died, and the next brother took the disease in a very dangerous form. The virulence of the plague was just at his height, and the father, mother, and brothers of the sick man all fled from him, and lodged elsewhere. There was one brother, however, who stayed behind, and would not leave his brother. His uncles and brothers all called to him, and urged him to follow them; and when he turned a deaf ear to their words, they exclaimed, " It is his nature not to fear disease." Then he nursed his brother, not closing his eyes night and day. Meanwhile he kept putting his hands on the coffins of the dead brothers, stooping over them and bemoaning their loss. This went on for more than one hundred days, until, the violence of the epidemic having abated, the members of the family came back. The sick man recovered, and the faithful brother took no harm.

XXVI.

The family of Yang or the Willows was
prosperous for many generations, elder and
younger brothers mutually helping and
serving like father and son.

The elder brother, "Sower of the Seed,"
had a stiff and stubborn temper; but his
brothers "Banian" and "Ferry" were gentle
and yielding.

The brothers were wont to meet early
each morning in the hall, and there they sat
all day long enjoying one another's company.
If there was anything specially nice to eat,
no one would taste of it till all three had sat
down. After they had reached the age of
sixty, "Banian" and "Ferry" both held
high office; but "Ferry" (the younger) still,
early and late, came to salute and inquire for
"Banian," the sons and nephews standing
respectfully in a row below the steps, and
"Ferry" would not venture to sit down till
"Banian" gave the sign.

After this the two younger brothers were
appointed to the charge of far sundered pro-

vinces ; but at the coming in of the pleasant
fruits of the four seasons, " Ferry " never
failed to despatch some to his brother by an
official messenger, and until he had done so
he would not taste them himself. " Banian,"
too, when he received these proofs of his
brother's love, wept over them.

XXVII.

A certain great officer had a younger
brother named " Perverse," who was con-
stantly getting intoxicated.

One day, when he was tipsy, he shot at
and killed his brother's ox which dragged his
cart. When the great man came home, his wife
met him, and said : " Perverse has shot your ox."

He did not seem surprised, nor did he ask
questions, but simply said : " Well, let it be
cut up for food;" and sat down quietly to
read. His wife exclaimed again :

" Perverse has shot the ox ; surely this is
no light matter !"

" I am aware of it," said her husband ; and
did not even change colour, but kept reading
his book.

XXVIII.

There were once two brothers of the Li or "Apricot" family. One was named "Light Doorway" and the younger "Light Brow." They were very friendly and loving together. "Light Brow" married before his elder brother, and their mother gave over the control of the house to "Light Brow's" wife.

After the old lady's death "Light Doorway" also married; and "Light Brow" sent his wife at once with the keys, account books, and stores, to hand over to her sister-in-law. "Light Doorway" returned them, saying: "My sister-in-law heretofore served our departed mother. It was our mother's command that she should have the control; and this wish must be held sacred." Then they fell on each other's necks, and wept.

XXIX.

There were once two brothers, the elder named Duke Peace, the younger Earl Bland, who lived together in peace and love.

When the elder was eighty years old, his brother honoured him as a venerable father; and took care of him as of a tender infant.

At every meal he asked him every other minute if his hunger was satisfied or no; and when the weather began to get chilly, he stroked his back, and said: "Are not your clothes too thin, brother?"

Why was this incessant care shown by Bland for Peace, as to his hunger and thirst, and cold and heat? Why, but that it is a rare thing in the world to have a brother, and a rarer thing still to have a white-haired brother?

"The fame of brother's love the breezes waft along,
Fit theme for eager thought, and laudatory song."

XXX.

A family named Brown had been long distinguished for harmony and love.

One of the brothers was on his way to the capital to compete for the highest degree. The rumour reached him that his elder brother was ill. He sighed, and said:

"Calamities are swift; honour can come by-and-by. I must go to my brother;" and so saying, he instantly turned back.

The next year he came out head of the whole list for admission to the Imperial Academy, the Han-lin (Forest of Pencils); the senior wrangler of his year.

XXXI.

Two brothers named Shang and Dzen went together to the war. One day during a fight Shang's horse was struck by an arrow and fell. His younger brother Dzen instantly dismounted, and gave his horse to Shang.

Shang exclaimed: "Why don't you save yourself?"

Dzen replied: "To forget one's self, to say *I* am not, is right; but one must never forget one's brother, or act as though *he* was not."

CHAPTER IV.

1. IF a man has not committed any deed that wounds his conscience, a knock may come at dead of night and he will not be startled.

2. The recompense for the good and for the bad is like the shadow following the form.

3. Gold is empty, silver vain ; after death, can they remain in the dead man's hand ?

4. Clear and plain is the road to heaven, but the multitude are unwilling to keep it.

5. If you build your house by hard dealing, the gain won't last long.

6. Man cannot have a thousand days of

prosperity : the flower cannot have a hundred days of bloom.

7. Think of your *own* faults the first part of the night (when you are awake), and of the faults of *others* the latter part of the night (when you are asleep).

8. Though the tree be a thousand yards high, the leaf must flutter down to the root.

9. The best and strongest man in the world finds it hard to escape from the two words " no continuance."

10. A life's work is like a spring dream.

" I think what a dream we live in, until it seems for the moment the saddest dream that ever was dreamed. What a dream it is, this work and strife ; and how little we do in the dream after all!"—*Letters of Charles Dickens.*

11. One spark can set a thousand hills in flame. (Compare St. James iii. 6.)

12. Riches and honour are like a dream; office and rank are like foam on the water.

13. One joy will disperse a hundred griefs.

(A striking proverb; but its great fulfilment the Chinese are ignorant of : the first moment in heaven outshining all the darkness of earth's sorrows.)

14. If you bear suffering upon suffering, you will soon rise step by step over other men.

> ". . . Men may rise on stepping-stones
>   Of their dead selves to higher things."

15. If you give out publicly, you will receive it back secretly. (A strange contrast this to our Lord's far higher saying, " Your Father which seeth in secret, Himself shall reward you openly.")

16. Good friends will settle accounts promptly.

17. Man must be sharpened by man ; the knife must be set on the stone. (Compare Proverbs xxvii. 17.)

18. If you wish your children's good, always let them be three-parts out of ten hungry and cold.

19. You may be uncivil to a great man ; but mind you are respectful to a small man.

20. You may offer clay loaves to Buddha (if only you first bribe the priest, that is).

21. To go on pilgrimage to offer incense in a distant temple, is not so good as showing kindness near home.   (Compare 1 Sam. xv. 22.)

22. New-come relations are eagerly welcomed ; old relations are thrown into the corner.

23. High heaven is not high ; man's heart is ever higher.

There is a striking parallel to this in Tennyson's " The Voice and the Peak," stanza viii. :

> " The Peak is high and flushed
>   At his highest with sunrise fire ;
> The Peak is high, and the stars are high,
>   And the thought of a man is higher."

24. Seek shade under the tall tree's boughs. (" No place like home;" as the Chinese explain this proverb.)

25. Let men despise me as they please. If Heaven spurns me not, then loss turns to gain.

26. To search for a needle in the great sea. (*Anglicè*, " in a bundle of hay.")

27. A long string will fly the kite high. (As we say, " A long purse can do anything.")

28. If you want to be happy, let great become small (make the best of difficulties or injuries).

29. A bad man is sure to meet with a worse to hurt him ; like the toad catching the stinging caterpillar.

This reminds one somewhat of the well-known verse :

" Great fleas have little fleas upon their backs to bite 'em,
And little fleas have lesser fleas, and so *ad infinitum*."

30. Better crack the drum than let the standard fall. (A noble proverb this, which may well be applied to the Church militant.)

31. Better be a bright (honest) beggar, than a muddy (dishonest) millionaire.

32. However enraged, don't go to law ; however poor, don't steal.

33. When sitting quietly, keep thinking of your own faults; when conversing with friends, don't talk of the faults of others.

34. A small boat must not have a heavy cargo. (Don't press a child beyond his powers.)

35. If you have money, and use it in charity, it won't be lost.

36. If you rear a tiger indoors, when it is full-grown it will eat you. (Compare Æschylus, Agam. 717:

"ἔθρεψεν δὲ λέοντα."—κ. τ. λ.)

37. The mouth is but as wind; the pen is proof (littera scripta manet).

38. To the hungry man all is good meat; to the thirsty man all is refreshing. (Hunger is the best sauce.)

39. Use men as you use wood. If one inch is rotten, you must not reject the whole piece.

40. If you have good children, you need not toil to build them houses.

CHAPTER V.

A QUARTER of a century ago, China was rent and torn by a great rebellion.

The object of the rebellion was to dethrone the present Tartar rulers, and to substitute for them a line of native Chinese emperors; and the name T'ai-p'ing or "Great Peace was what the rebels chose for their proposed rule. During the fifteen years of the struggle they brought, however, nothing but great confusion and misery to the country.

The leader, Hung-sew-tseuen, and his first band of followers, seem in their early days to have had no thought of rebellion; but rather, influenced by the teaching of missionaries

5

and by the study of the Bible and religious tracts, they were deeply convinced of the wickedness of the world, of the folly of idolatry, and of the truth and sovereignty of God. They used to meet at night on lofty hill-tops for prayer, and for the reception of converts into their little band, which they called " The Society of Worshippers of God."

After this, partly through disappointment in his attempts to attain a literary degree, and partly through the swelling of his company by " every one who was in debt, or in distress, or discontented," and by many also who had already been rebels, Hung-sew-tseuen openly took up arms against the Government in 1850, and marched northwards from the neighbourhood of Canton, till, in 1853, he seized Nanking, or the " Southern Capital," as the name means. His generals then pressed further northwards, with the hope of capturing Peking, the " Northern Capital," and so annihilating the Tartar rule.

The tide of war swept onwards, till the rebels were within a hundred miles of their goal ; and then, after this wonderful and terrible march of more than a thousand miles from Canton to T'ien-tsin, they were checked by the Tartar horsemen, and retreated to Nanking.

In 1861 the T'ai-p'ings invaded the province of Cheh-keang, and devastated nearly every part of that beautiful country with fire and sword. The poor people fled in hopeless confusion. Some of them hid in the hills. I climbed, in February, 1879, a hill nearly three thousand feet high, called the " Horse-course Ridge "—a noble mass of mountain, faced with a craggy wall of rock, and beyond the wall a level summit on which a horse can gallop. Up this steep mountain the poor women and children toiled ; but even to this " high rock " the murderous rebels pursued them.

In some places, however, the country people stood their ground against the foe. In the Chu-ki region, about fifty miles south of Hangchow (the capital of Cheh-keang), with one or two rusty cannon and rude stockades, they managed to keep the whole T'ai-p'ing host at bay for many months, and nearly ten thousand of the rebels are said to have been killed before they succeeded in overpowering this hill fortress. When at last they *did* succeed, all the fury of revenge was, of course, let loose, and everyone who could move fled as from certain death. It was useless to enter Hangchow, for that city was held strongly by the T'ai-p'ings, and everyone was flying from that neighbourhood also.

The natives of Hangchow assert that during these two terrible years of their misery, the great "bore,"* which I have seen many times since heaving and lashing the river Tsientang into a dangerous confusion of waves, did not once appear; a special mercy from heaven, as they believe, permitting thus the poor fugitives to cross the river on their way to Ningpo without the danger of shipwreck.

Ningpo is the chief seaport of Cheh-keang, and having a settlement of European mer-

* A dangerous wave caused by the meeting of the stream and tide at the mouth of certain rivers.

chants and missionaries, with some promise
of safety, this was the place to which most
of the refugees directed their flight.

Amongst the crowd in the year 1862
might have been seen a thin half-starved
widow woman with her two sons, aged twelve
and seven. She reached Ningpo in safety,
and lived there for several years; and there
she heard the Gospel, and was baptised
about the year 1871 by Mr. Gough, when
the name Naomi was given her. The elder
son became a soldier, and the younger,
named Ah-ts'ih or " Number Seven," went
back with his mother to their ruined home,
and began to till again the few fields which
had so long lain fallow, and to earn again, as
his father earned before him, a livelihood by
burning charcoal, which forms one of the
chief employments of the men in that part
of the country. Their home lay in a little
village far in the recesses of the hills, named
Yang-kia-woo, or " The Lake of the Yang
family." A massive range of hills shuts
them in from the river, and from the more

populous parts of the Chu-ki district.   These
hills are said to harbour tigers and leopards,
but the Buddhists have a large monastery at
the top, and seem to live there without fear.
The highest of these hills has a curious
legend connected with it.   An ancient emperor is said to have tried to move this hill,
and as it was stubborn and refused to obey
him, in his wrath he sheared off its summit
with his sword; and they show you, at a
town which I have often passed, a mass of
rock, which is said to be the fallen brow of
the stubborn hill.

During old Naomi's residence in Ningpo,
and before she became a Christian, she betrothed a little girl as the future wife of
" Number Seven," and when she returned to
her distant home, she was very glad to leave
this little girl under our charge in a mission
boarding-school at Ningpo.   We found the
little thing very obedient and tractable; but
she had a very weak constitution, and she
was often so seriously ill as to make us very
anxious.   She made good progress with

her lessons, however; and when still under
twelve years of age she could repeat by heart
all four Gospels. One day old Naomi appeared with her eldest son, and told us, to
our surprise and sorrow, that they had come
to fetch the poor girl away. We reasoned
with the old woman. We pointed out to her
that her little daughter-in-law was too young
to be married to Ah-ts'ih, and that her
attacks of illness would be more frequent
and more serious in her poor home without
the good food and medical care which we
could provide for her in the school.

"Yes," she replied, "I know that well, and
I am quite of your mind; but my sons insist
upon the girl going home, and I cannot
prevent it."

All that we could do was to prevail
upon them to delay their departure for
ten days. When our little scholar heard
what was to happen, she wept very much,
and earnestly desired to be baptised before
she left. After careful preparation and ex-
amination she was baptised in our school

chapel by the name Ruth; and notwithstanding her great reserve and timidity, we had good hope of her simple faith and sincere desire to serve the Saviour.

The next day (taking with her a precious parcel of Chinese books—a New Testament, a prayer-book and a hymn-book, two small volumes of sermons, the "Peep of Day," "Line upon Line," and a Christian story-book), this little Chinese Ruth followed this Chinese Naomi to dwell where she dwelt. The people of far-off Yang-kia-woo should be her people; but they were both fully determined that the true God, and not the idols of Yang-kia-woo, should henceforth be their God (Ruth i. 16, 17).

For nearly two years we lost sight of our little Ruth. "There was she buried," we might almost say, so far as our knowledge of her welfare and Christian progress was concerned. They had promised to write to us and to pay us occasional visits; but their extreme poverty and the difficulty of communication prevented it.

In the spring of 1876 we moved from Ningpo to Hangchow, and I then found that the remote region where Ruth was supposed to be living was more accessible from Hangchow than from Ningpo. I obtained from Mr. Gough the name of the village and its bearings from the district city, Chu-ki; and after many inquiries from natives of that region, whom I met in Hangchow, I started with a Chinese guide on a four days' journey in search of our lost sheep.

Embarking from Hangchow at noon on the broad bosom of the great Tsien-tang, which flows past the city in a stream two miles wide, we turned southwards up a branch which joins the main river about fifteen miles from the anchorage; and that night we caught sight of the tiger-haunted and irate-emperor-shaken mountain top, with the light of the Buddhist monastery twinkling in the gloom. The next morning we were in the Chu-ki district, and I saw from afar the white walls of the mountain fortress, which the hardy people of these hills and plains held so long against the rebels.   Our boat tracked slowly against the stream, now shallowing as we approached its source.   We jumped on shore from time to time, and asked for Yang-kia-woo.

" There it is," replied a man, basking in the morning sunshine; " those houses in front of you, the other side of the stream, are Yang-kia-woo!   Yes," he continued, as we further questioned him; " yes, now you mention it, I think there *is* a girl living there who stayed in Ningpo with her mother-in-law for some time.   Go in and inquire."

We went in eagerly, but the villagers stared at us vacantly for a while, and then told us that no one of that name or description lived there.

I imagined that they were suspicious of me as a foreigner, so I retired to the boa and left the Chinese guide to parley alone; but he soon rejoined we with the assurance that the people we were in search of were not there.

We inquired on that day and the next in

two other places with similar names, but all in vain; and I was obliged to return to Hangchow with a heavy heart. A month later I sent down a Christian Chinese, a native of the Chu-ki region, to search alone, but he too returned unsuccessful.

In the autumn of that year I was cheered by the news that at last " Number Seven " had been seen and the village discovered. I sent my Chinese guide down first to reconnoitre, and he returned, having seen Naomi and Ruth alive and well. But he feared that they had relapsed, however unwillingly, into idolatry. He saw the usual idolatrous charm papers, one red and one green, pasted on the house door; and over the oven where poor Ruth was cooking, a picture of the kitchen god, a favourite object of worship, was fastened; and he brought back the rumour that old Naomi's heathen sons forbade the reading of the Bible and prayer to the true God.

As soon as I could leave home I started myself for Ruth's distant village. It was a

long journey of twenty-six miles from my
boat to Yang-kia-woo, and back again at
night, and part of the way I rode in a
primitive kind of sedan chair. It looked like
a great tray, with a rim round it a foot high.
I sat or lay in this tray, and it was carried
dangling from a stout pole which rested on
the shoulders of the two bearers—one in
front, one behind. As the weight was con-
siderable, they rested the pole on forked
sticks shod with iron every two or three
hundred yards, and shifted the strain from
shoulder to shoulder.

The scenery, as I went further into the
heart of the country, was very beautiful, and
clear running streams reminded me every
now and then of Dorset and Devon. At
last, after crossing the shoulder of a low hill,
I saw the outskirts of Yang-kia-woo, and we
soon entered the village street. As we
walked up it, I at once recognised our long-
lost Ruth washing greens in the stream.
She caught sight of us and ran in ; but her
sister-in-law welcomed us at the house-door,

and on that door, alas! I saw only too plainly the idolatrous charms. Old Naomi was sitting inside, oppressed with a bad cough, and suffering from the effects of a fall downstairs. Little Ruth retired into the further end of the cottage, feeling shy and timid before the crowd which gathered quickly to see the strange apparition of a foreigner in this remote village, where none had ever been before. Soon the neighbours began to talk; and I was touched and deeply interested to hear from them things which showed that our little scholar had not wholly gone back into idolatry, nor hidden her light entirely under a bushel.

Timid as she was, with a feeble-minded though professedly Christian mother-in-law with a heathen husband, and the rest of the family all heathen, without Christian friends, and neither church nor school at hand, she was yet, as the neighbours told me, in the habit of going upstairs alone to read and pray; and she had spoken about the Lord Jesus to her sister-in-law. Presently

"Number Seven" came in, and I charged
him with unfilial conduct in compelling his
mother against her conscience to connive at
idolatry.   He smiled, and laid the blame on
his elder brother.   I then called to Ruth,
and after long hesitation she was induced to
come forward; and at my suggestion she
climbed the rickety stairs slowly with her
tiny stunted feet, and brought down her
precious books.   I opened the New Testament at St. John iii. 16—21, and told her to
read.   She did so, clearly and well, and I
found that she had forgotten very little
during the two or three years which had
passed since her last lesson in our school.   I
was glad indeed for the crowd to hear the
wonderful words read by one of themselves.
When Ruth had finished, one of the bystanders exclaimed : " How foolish of *you* to
be ashamed !   It is *we* who have reason to
blush, who cannot read a word."   I en-
couraged Ruth after this to read from her
New Testament whenever the women had
time to come into her cottage and listen.

I left the place again after dinner, with the promise that Ruth and Naomi should come up to Hangchow on a visit, and that idolatry should no longer be forced in any way on these poor Christians.

To our glad surprise—for promises are not always kept in China—Naomi, " Number Seven," and Ruth all appeared on the day appointed ; and Ruth spent a month with us to perfect her reading. We found, too, that she had remembered enough of her writing to compose a Chinese letter, with a little help from us, to a kind friend in England.

The soldier-brother visited us also, and attended morning and evening prayers in our house. The idolatrous pictures were, we heard, removed from their house ; and when Ah-ts'ih came to bid us farewell before we left for England, he expressed some desire himself to become a Christian.

Good comes out of evil again and again through God's wonder-working Providence. Fresh grass and fragrant flowers spring up and smile after the devastation of a thunderstorm. And the tremendous horrors of the Chinese rebellion, which drove Naomi to Ningpo to fetch thence her little Ruth, have brought forth, we trust, one peaceable fruit which shall yet multiply in far-off Yang-kia-woo.

THE END.

BILLING AND SONS, PRINTERS AND ELECTROTYPERS, GUILDFORD.